The Kingdom of Wrenly

16

The Dream Portal

By Jordan Quinn
Illustrated by Robert McPhillips

LITTLE SIMON

New York   London   Toronto   Sydney   New Delhi

LITTLE SIMON

An imprint of Simon & Schuster Children's Publishing Division
1230 Avenue of the Americas, New York, New York 10020
First Little Simon paperback edition May 2021
Copyright © 2021 by Simon & Schuster, Inc.
Also available in a Little Simon hardcover edition.
All rights reserved, including the right of reproduction in whole or in part in any form.
LITTLE SIMON is a registered trademark of Simon & Schuster, Inc., and associated colophon is a trademark of Simon & Schuster, Inc.
For information about special discounts for bulk purchases, please contact
Simon & Schuster Special Sales at 1-866-506-1949 or business@simonandschuster.com.
The Simon & Schuster Speakers Bureau can bring authors to your live event. For more information or to book an event contact the Simon & Schuster Speakers Bureau at 1-866-248-3049 or visit our website at www.simonspeakers.com.
Manufactured in the United States of America 0421 MTN
2 4 6 8 10 9 7 5 3 1
This book has been cataloged with the Library of Congress.
ISBN 978-1-5344-9551-7 (hc)
ISBN 978-1-5344-9550-0 (pbk)
ISBN 978-1-5344-9552-4 (eBook)

CONTENTS

CHAPTER 1

Dream
Weaver

Clara Gills stood in the village of the kingdom of Wrenly.

What am I doing here? she wondered. *I know I came here for a reason, but what was it?* She couldn't seem to remember.

The streets were empty. The shops were shuttered, and there wasn't a single street vendor to be seen.

"HELLO?" Clara called. "Anybody?"

Nobody answered.

The entire land was quiet . . . too quiet.

Clara looked toward the castle where her best friend, Prince Lucas, lived. A dark blue-and-pink mist hung over the castle. The mist swirled wildly, and the castle seemed strangely run-down and haunted.

With a gasp, Clara cupped her hand over her mouth. *There must be some kind of strange magic at work!* she thought. She quickly ran to her father's bakery and found the front door wide open.

Inside, loaves of bread lined the shelves and counters, like normal.

Clara sniffed the air. Instead of smelling fresh bread, the bakery smelled musty and stale. She picked up a loaf of bread. It was rock-hard and dotted with fuzzy green spots.

"Mold?!" she said. "My father would *never* sell moldy bread!"

Then Clara realized her father was nowhere to be seen. She dropped the stale bread and raced up the lane toward the castle. She had to find Lucas. Something was very, very wrong.

As she turned a corner, Clara spotted the prince's red dragon trotting in the street.

"Ruskin!" Clara called, but the dragon ignored her.

"RUSKIN!" she shouted again at
the top of her voice.

Still the dragon walked on, so
Clara chased after him.

When she reached Ruskin, something strange happened.

The ground beneath Clara's feet
began to tremble and shake. Cracks
splintered in every direction. Then,
all at once, the entire street split
apart . . . and Clara tumbled into
the opening.

"*HELP!*" she cried.

Clara reached out and grabbed hold of a ledge. Her feet dangled over open air, and her fingers began to slip.

"RUSKIN! *PLEASE HELP!*" she hollered.

Looking up, Clara saw the scarlet dragon peek over the ledge and stare down at her from above. His eyes glowed with fire.

"CLARA!" Ruskin called. "WAKE UP!"

Clara sat up in her own bed. As she caught her breath, she smelled fresh bread baking downstairs. *Oh, phew!* she thought. *It was only a dream! But it felt so real!*

Then Clara spied a red dragon curled at the foot of her bed.

It was Ruskin.

CHAPTER 2

A Shared Dream

"Ruskin, what are *you* doing here?!"

Clara's cry startled Ruskin. He shot off the bed and flew smack into Clara's bookshelf.

Wump! The books tumbled onto the floor. Then the bookshelf fell on top of the pile. Ruskin scampered into a corner.

Clara shook her head. "Are you okay?"

Ruskin whimpered. Clara hopped out of bed and ran to his side. She patted him on the head.

"Shhh, it's all right," she said calmly. "Now, how did you get in here?"

Ruskin shrugged.

"Of course you can't tell me. You can't talk," Clara said with a chuckle. "Well, let's get you back to the castle. Lucas must be looking for you."

After getting dressed, Clara walked Ruskin home. This time the streets were full of vendors and shoppers. It didn't look anything like the creepy world she had seen in her dream.

But something still seemed off. Clara noticed that the townspeople looked tired. Everyone had dark circles under their eyes. The shop owners yawned, and the goblin rug vendor had fallen asleep on top of his rugs.

The same thing was true at the castle. Everyone looked tired.

One of the guards at the front gate had even nodded off. It was as if nobody had gotten a good night's rest except Ruskin.

Ruskin bounded into the castle with his normal zip. Clara followed him directly to the dragon's favorite place . . . the kitchen. She thought Lucas might be there eating his breakfast. But no luck.

"The prince is already in his work-  shop," said Cook with a yawn. "He's working on some- thing top secret."

Clara thanked Cook and headed to the workshop. Ruskin stayed behind for breakfast.

While walking down the hall, she wondered what Lucas could be working on.

She didn't want to barge in, so when she arrived, she knocked on the door. "It's CLARA!" she called as she heard rustling.

"Hang on!" said the prince. "Okay, come in!"

Clara opened the door and saw the prince standing in front of a

workbench covered with a blanket. She spied something sticking out on one side. It looked like a dragon wing.

Lucas quickly covered it up. "Hey, no peeking! I want my new invention to be a surprise!"

Clara rolled her eyes. "Okay, okay! No peeking, but listen to this."

She told Lucas about her dream and how she had woken up with Ruskin sleeping at the foot of her bed.

"That *is* weird," the prince said. "I wonder why Ruskin slept at your house. He's never done that before."

Clara shrugged. "I'm more worried about my dream. Do you think it could've been real?"

Lucas laughed. "Of course not, silly! It was only a *dream*."

CHAPTER 3

A Nightmare

That night Ruskin slept in Lucas's room.

Unfortunately, Lucas could not fall asleep at all. He kept thinking about his invention. It was so close to being finished. After tossing and turning for hours, the prince finally hopped out of bed to work on it.

He called for Ruskin to join him, but the dragon was gone.

Lucas raced out of his room and checked Ruskin's favorite hiding spots: the kitchen, the larder, and the dragon lair. But there was no sign of Ruskin.

The missing dragon wasn't the only weird thing going on. The entire castle was eerily empty! Lucas couldn't even find his mother and father, the queen and king!

Something is terribly wrong, the prince thought.

Then Lucas heard a sound. It was a low, steady hum mixed with hisses and sizzles, like when Cook used a very hot griddle. But this sound wasn't coming from the kitchen. It was coming from the prince's workshop!

Lucas slowly opened the door to discover Ruskin standing in front of Lucas's covered invention.

The sound in the room was extremely loud. Lucas had to cover his ears to block the noise! It was coming from a very strange crack in the wall.

He studied the crack and saw that it wasn't actually *in* the wall. The rip was in the air itself! A blue-and-pink mist began to swirl out and fill the air.

"Ruskin, what's going on?!" Lucas screamed over the noise.

The scarlet dragon didn't answer him. Instead, Ruskin tore the cover off Lucas's invention with one of his claws.

"Lucas, you *must* make the wings lighter," his dragon said. "If you ever hope to save me, *fix* the wings."

"What are you talking about?" Lucas asked. "Why would I need to save you?"

The mist from the opening moved past the prince and circled around his dragon.

"I'm *not* safe," Ruskin said. "Now wake up, Lucas! Wake up before it's too late!"

Lucas sat up in bed and gasped for air. The hum from his dream still rang in his ears.

Then the prince noticed *another* opening in the air . . . only this time it wasn't a dream. . . . It was *real*.

And Ruskin was walking right toward it.

CHAPTER 4

A Daymare

Lucas leaped out of bed and threw himself in between Ruskin and the swirling mist.

"STOP!" he screamed.

But the dragon's eyes were closed, and he was only focused on the misty opening. Ruskin was in a trance.

"Ruskin, PLEASE!" Lucas begged as he scanned the room for something, *anything*, to wake the dragon up.

Lucas pulled a chair into his path, but Ruskin nudged it aside. Next Lucas tried to push against the dragon's shoulders, but Ruskin was determined to walk into the mist.

What is going on? Lucas wondered.

It's almost as if Ruskin is being controlled by that mist!

Then Ruskin opened his jaws, and Lucas saw a small fire growing in the dragon's throat. Would his own dragon actually attack him with fire?

Quickly Lucas reached for his last hope . . . a sack of chocolate-covered pretzels that  he frantically waved in front of his friend.

Finally Ruskin paused. His nose twitched at the delicious smell. Then his eyes opened, and the dragon lunged for the pretzels.

With the trance broken, the mist disappeared completely.

Lucas fell to his knees beside Ruskin, who was chomping away at the sweet treats. "That was a close call, boy! It's a good thing you love food."

But Lucas had a feeling the danger had only just begun.

CHAPTER 5

The Dream Portal

The next morning a royal letter was waiting for Clara.

Come to the castle as soon as you wake up! HURRY! I'll be in the kitchen.

Thanks,

Lucas

PRINCE LUCAS

Chickens scattered and clucked as Clara raced out the door and down the street to meet her friend.

In the royal kitchen she found Ruskin resting in a cage, munching strawberries.

"What's Ruskin doing in there?"

Lucas held up a finger. "I'll tell you in a sec. But first, Cook, could you please keep Ruskin's cage filled with his favorite foods? If he stops eating, send for me at once!"

Cook chuckled and pulled out a large pan. "Of course, my prince! Operation: Feed the Beast begins now."

Lucas thanked Cook and waved to Clara. "We have to go to the royal library *right now!*" he warned.

Clara watched as Lucas left the room without her. She knew that meant something *big* was up.

As they hurried down the hallway, Lucas told Clara about his dream and how the castle had been empty except for Ruskin. He also described the mysterious hum that had come from the opening in the air.

It sounded awful to Clara.

"Ruskin spoke to me in my dream," the prince explained. "And he used *words*—just like he did with *you*. He said he was in some kind of danger."

"That *does* seem a lot like my dream!" Clara gasped.

Lucas nodded. "That's not all. After I woke up, the swirling mist appeared *again*—only this time it was *real*. Ruskin was in a trance and being drawn to the opening. If I hadn't woken him up, he would have gone in!"

Clara shook her head in disbelief. "We need to find some answers!"

The kids got to work in the royal library. Lucas pored over books about the strange and unknown. Clara read up on the legends and lore of Wrenly. None of the books mentioned anything about a blue-and-pink swirling cloud in the air.

Then Clara picked up a fairy tale called *The Dream Portal of Wrenly*. "Isn't a portal a gateway between one world and another?" she asked.

Lucas set aside a book on storm clouds. "It is. Why?"

"Check this out," Clara said as she read aloud. "'There once was a Dream Portal built by fairies and wizards. The portal lay beyond Bogburp, where no one goes. Marked by an ancient circle of stones, a swirling blue-and-pink magic *mist* awaits the dreamers of Wrenly.'"

Lucas's eyes grew wide. "What did the Dream Portal do?"

Clara turned the page. "According to this, it was created to send sweet dreams to Wrenly. But the portal was overcome by a dark magic, and it sent forth nightmares instead. Everyone became too afraid to fall asleep!"

Lucas leaned closer. "So what happened?"

Clara skimmed to the end of the book. "The portal was closed by a goblin child who wasn't fooled by nightmares. Today all that remains is the circle of stones on a barren hillside."

Lucas stood up. "It sounds like the Dream Portal is back!"

Clara raised an eyebrow. "But aren't fairy tales *pretend*?"

The prince nodded. "They're *supposed* to be pretend, but we've read through stacks of books, and this is the only one that describes

the mist from both our dreams. And did your dream feel *pretend*? Did the swirling mist or Ruskin's voice or the sense that something bad was going to happen feel *pretend*?"

"Definitely *not*," Clara admitted. "You're right, the Dream Portal *is* back. And for some reason, it wants Ruskin."

CHAPTER 6

A Dream Key

Lucas and Clara hurried back to the kitchen to find a terrible scene. Cook was sound asleep, curled up inside the cage where Ruskin had been. A light mist encircled him.

"Cook! Wake up!" Lucas snapped.

But the giant chef did not stir. Instead, his snores shook the room.

Clara wasted no time searching for their friend.

She tossed pots and pans aside before announcing, "Ruskin's *gone!*"

They quickly ran into the great hall and found a castle-guard.

"Have you seen Ruskin?" the prince asked breathlessly.

"Sure, I just saw him on my rounds," the guard said as she pointed toward the West Tower. "He was yawning by the battlement."

Lucas and Clara thanked the guard and charged toward the stairs. As soon as they stepped onto the wall-walk, they spotted Ruskin stretching his wings.

"Ruskin!" Lucas cried as he and Clara ran toward the dragon. "We were so worried you might have been—"

But before the prince could finish his sentence, Ruskin finished it for him.

"*Asleep?*" the dragon said in a deep, groggy voice.

Ruskin was back in a trance. His eyes were open, but they had the fiery glow the kids had seen in their dreams. This was not the Ruskin that Lucas knew.

"Who are you?" demanded the prince.

"I am the Dream Portal," said the voice coming from Ruskin. "And I have waited years for a scarlet dragon. Your Ruskin is very powerful and very pesky. He was able to break into your dreams and save you, after all. But in showing me his power, he gave away his secret. Using him, I can unlock the dreams of every living creature in the kingdom. Then, once inside, I will be able to control *all* of Wrenly!"

The Dream Portal let out an evil laugh as it forced Ruskin to fly away.

"*Nooooooo!*" Lucas and Clara cried.

Clara grabbed the prince by the arm. "It's escaping to the Dream Portal! We've got to stop them. But how can we outrace a flying dragon if we travel on horseback?"

Lucas turned and ran toward the stairs. "I've got something faster than horses! Follow me!"

The kids ran to the workshop, where Lucas ripped the cover off his invention.

"This is my dragon-flyer!" he announced. "I put the finishing touches on it this morning!"

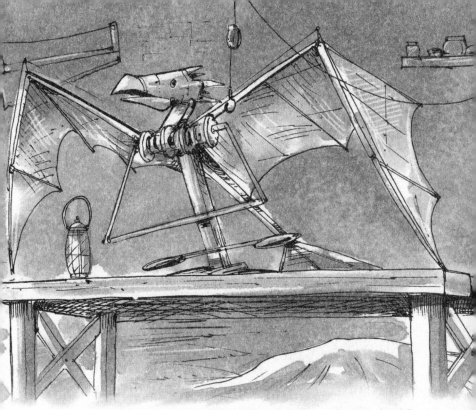

The dragon-flyer had the head of a dragon, dragon wings, and a bar to hang from and steer.

"Whoa," said Clara, impressed. "What gave you the idea to build this?"

"I wanted to fly with Ruskin," Lucas admitted. "Feel like taking a test-drive?"

Clara smiled. "I thought you'd never ask."

The kids carried the dragon-flyer to the castle tower. It was very light. Then they strapped themselves into their harnesses, grabbed hold of the frame, and leaped into the air.

CHAPTER 7

Lucas's Dream Machine

The dragon-flyer swooped and swerved as the kids struggled to control the invention.

"Lucas, watch out for that flagpole!" Clara shouted.

Lucas dodged sideways as people beneath them pointed upward in amazement.

The kids shifted their weight until each wing was perfectly balanced.

Then Lucas pointed the nose of the dragon downward so the wind would flow over the surface of the wings.

The dragon-flyer began to speed forward. Then it began to rise.

"This is so wild!" Clara cried as she searched the sky for Ruskin. The red dragon had gotten a huge head start.

"I know!" Lucas said. "I never thought I was building it for a rescue mission!"

The two friends soared over farms, rivers, and forests. Wrenly looked like a patchwork quilt from on high.

Then Clara spied something in the distance and pointed. "Could that red speck be Ruskin?"

Lucas squinted in the direction of Clara's finger.

"It's definitely Ruskin!" he said. "I'd know that tail anywhere."

They moved closer and closer, but then Ruskin quickly changed course and flew high up into a cloud.

"Uh-oh, we've been spotted!" Lucas cried. "The Dream Portal is trying to lose us in that cloud."

Clara tightened her grip on the bar. "Then we'll have to fly *through* the cloud!"

Lucas lifted the dragon-flyer higher and higher. Soon they entered the cloud where Ruskin had disappeared. But Lucas began to lose control of his steering.

"Everything's white!" he cried. "I can't tell which way is up and which way is down!"

As they flipped upside down, a hole opened in the cloud.

"Quick! There!" Clara said.

Lucas guided the dragon-flyer out of the cloud. Now they were safe, but Ruskin was gone.

"We lost the trail!" complained the prince.

Clara thought for a moment. "The book said the Dream Portal was on the other side of Bogburp. Let's head there!"

"Yeah!" cheered Lucas. "But how do we know where we are?"

Clara studied the ground. "There's the village of Trellis. If we head east now, we'll be on course for Bogburp."

Lucas let out a sigh. "Thanks, Clara. I don't know what I would do without you!"

Then he shifted the dragon-flyer eastward and hoped they would be in time to save their friend.

CHAPTER 8

The Dream Team

Glub!

Glub!

Glurp!

The swamps of Bogburp bubbled with stench and steam. Clara pinched her nose. "It smells like rotten eggs!"

Lucas nodded. "That's why it's the perfect barrier to the Dream Portal," he said.

The prince took a deep breath and held it the rest of the way across Bogburp. When the land turned back to meadows, the two friends breathed normally again.

"Lucas, look up ahead," Clara cried. "It's that swirling blue-and-pink mist we saw in our dreams!"

Lucas steered toward the mist
and saw a circle of glittering black
stones—just like they had read about
in the fairy tale.

"It's the rock formation!" he said.

But Clara wasn't looking at the
ground. She was looking up in the sky.

"It's Ruskin!" she called out.

The dragon was in a nosedive, flying headfirst into the mist.

"We have to go after him!" Lucas said.

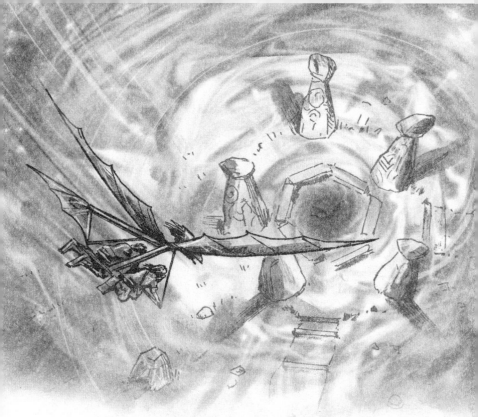

Clara nodded as Lucas aimed the dragon-flyer toward the mist at the heart of the rock formation and squeezed her eyes tight.

They had entered the Dream Portal.

Instead of seeing another world, Lucas woke up in his own bed with Ruskin nestled by his feet. The prince scratched his head.

Okay, what's going on? he thought. *Was I dreaming again?*

Then he heard a knock on his door.

"Prince Lucas?" It was Sherman, the prince's personal attendant. "Your presence is required in the great hall."

Lucas hopped out of bed. "Be right there!"

The prince ran to his closet. Hanging on the back of the door was a scarlet suit of armor—the same color as Ruskin. It had a note pinned to it.

Lucas,

This is your BIG day. To be the part, you must dress the part.

Love,

Mom and Dad

Lucas put on the armor and admired himself in the mirror. *Wow, this must be a very special occasion,* he thought.

Trumpets blared as Lucas and Ruskin entered the great hall. The hall was packed with people. Lucas and Ruskin were ushered to the top of a platform. The prince stood next to his father and mother, King Caleb and Queen Tasha.

Then his father made a royal proclamation.

"Hear ye! Hear ye! Today my son, Lucas, will be crowned king of Wrenly!"

CHAPTER 9

Broken
Dreams

Thwap!
Thwap!
Thwap!

Clara awoke to the sound of dragon wings beating outside her window. This time it wasn't Ruskin who had come to visit. It was Firestorm—her team partner from when she had joined the Knight Spires of Wrenly.

Clara leaned outside and, to her surprise, found *all* the Knight Spires waiting for her.

"Greetings, Thirteenth Knight! It is a glorious day in the kingdom of Wrenly," the Head Spire said. "We must get to the castle without delay!"

What is happening? wondered Clara. "I'll be right there!" she said.

Clara ran to her closet and found a suit of armor hanging on her door— just like Lucas had! Only, her suit of armor was made of shimmering yellow-and-green dragon scales.

Once in the armor, Clara ran to the window and clicked her tongue, and Firestorm flew in close.

She leaped onto her back and called out, "To the castle!"

And Firestorm lifted Clara above the rooftops.

Everyone in the kingdom had gathered in the castle's great hall, from townspeople and wizards to trolls and fairies. Clara took her place in the crowd and waved to the king and queen standing on the platform.

When the trumpets sounded, Lucas and Ruskin were led onto the platform. The Head Spire bent down and whispered something in Clara's ear.

"Today the prince will be crowned king!" he said. "And you will be his protector of the kingdom."

A wave of happiness swept over Clara. *Wow,* she thought. *Could this really be happening?*

King Caleb held up his crown. The crowd roared, and a feeling of fear rushed over Clara that washed away her joy.

"NOOOO!" she shouted. But the cheers of the crowd drowned out her wail. When the cheers died down, she tried again.

"LUCAS!" she yelled. "LUCAS!"

The prince looked over the crowd and met her eyes.

"It's a TRAP!" Clara shouted. "YOU MUST WAKE UP!"

The king began to lower his crown onto Lucas's head. But the prince held up his arm and blocked him.

Suddenly the room shook, and all the people around Lucas, Clara, and Ruskin burst into mist! A shock wave rushed around them, and then the three friends found themselves all alone in a place of darkness.

"You know what that *was*?" Clara cried. "It was the Dream Portal controlling our minds with a good dream!"

The prince looked at his arms and chest. His suit of armor was gone! His eyes flashed with anger.

"Nobody controls the kingdom of Wrenly except my father!" he said.

Then the same evil voice that had spoken through Ruskin began to speak to them.

"You're *wrong*, Prince Lucas!" the voice boomed. "The Dream Portal controls *everyone* and *everything*—including *you!*"

Lucas and Clara looked around but saw no one.

"I showed you a good dream," the Dream Portal continued. "Now it's time for a NIGHTMARE!"

Wake Up!

The friends huddled together.

"Prepare for anything!" Lucas whispered.

But nothing could prepare them for what happened next.

All at once Ruskin began to thrash his head from side to side. He backed away from his friends. Then his whole body began to shudder and shake.

"Ruskin, are you OKAY?" cried Clara.

Ruskin was changing. His body grew larger and larger. His teeth became long, frightening fangs. His claws curved into thick, sharp needles, and fury swirled in his eyes.

"ROOOOOOOOAAAAARRRR!" Ruskin screeched with fire streaming from his jaws.

Lucas and Clara grabbed hold of each other. The dragon's neck whipped back and forth. He roared again and split open the darkness. The kids were back in the great hall, but now stones tumbled onto the floor. A bust of King Caleb fell from its pedestal and shattered.

"Fight me!" bellowed Ruskin. "Or I will DESTROY both of you!"

Lucas scrambled on top of the pedestal to get closer to his dragon.

He stood tall and pushed out his chest.

"We will NOT fight you! And you will NOT destroy us!" he declared.

But Ruskin only grew larger until his head broke through the roof of the castle.

"I am TOO powerful for you!" Ruskin thundered as he looked down at them. "YOU CANNOT STOP ME!"

Lucas stared into the monster's eyes.

"You have NO power!" he shouted. "Because I know you're NOT real! None of this is real! It's only a dream! WAKE UP, Ruskin!"

Ruskin paused and shook his head in confusion.

"Keep talking!" Clara cried. "I think you're reaching the REAL Ruskin!"

Lucas took a breath and spoke to his friend. "Remember the games we played when you were a hatchling? Remember how we used to raid the royal kitchen at night? Try to think of our adventures together!"

Ruskin roared again—only this time he began to shrink. Lucas kept talking about the fun times they'd had together. The more the prince talked, the smaller Ruskin became. Soon Ruskin was back to his normal size.

Lucas jumped off the pedestal
and raced toward his dragon. Clara
ran over too. The three best friends
hugged one another.

"Let's get out of this dream!"
Lucas urged.

"STOP!" thundered the voice of the Dream Portal. "The dragon is the price for your freedom! Give him to me!"

The Dream Portal would never grant freedom to anyone—no matter what it was given. So Ruskin grabbed his friends and took flight.

"Ruskin will *never* be yours!" cried the prince.

Lightning bolts flashed. Thunder exploded and rumbled. A magical storm was brewing.

Ruskin squawked and flew straight into the dark clouds. The air crackled and popped with electricity. Lucas and Clara shut their eyes and held on tightly. Ruskin picked up speed. His body shook violently as he powered through the storm.

KA-BOOM! Ruskin broke through the Dream Portal's storm barrier and into the sunshine.

Lucas whooped and looked back at where they'd flown from. The swirling mist faded away, like sun burning through the fog on Mermaid's Cove. Soon all that was left of the Dream Portal was a circle of ordinary rocks.

Ruskin touched down in a meadow of wildflowers. Lucas and Clara jumped off his back and rolled onto the ground. They laughed and whistled in relief. Then Lucas sat up suddenly.

"Oh no!" he cried.

"What is it?" asked Clara.

Lucas jumped up and said, "I left my dragon-flyer in the Dream Portal!"

Both Clara and Ruskin stared at the prince.

"Are you kidding?" questioned Clara. "We just saved the kingdom, and all you can think about is your lost dragon-flyer?"

Ruskin humphed in agreement.

Lucas shrugged. "But I worked really hard on it!"

Clara laughed. "Well, you can always *dream* up a new one . . . !" she said.

Lucas grabbed a clump of flowers and threw it at Clara.

Then the three friends fell over and closed their eyes for a nap.

It had been quite a day.